Variations of Labor

ISBN: 9781634059770

First [1] edition

Paperback original

Publisher:
Chin Music Press
1501 Pike Place #329
Seattle, WA 98101
www.chinmusicpress.com

Variations of Labor
Poems & Stories

by Alex Gallo-Brown

"You know, you really ought to be allowed to pick your own place to be born in. Considering how it gets into you."

Joseph Bell, Out of this Furnace

"This city hardly exists. It certainly does not exist as does our family, our friends, and our neighborhood."

Delmore Schwartz, "The World is a Wedding"

"Some cities glory in their culture, some in their institutions, some in their industries, but Seattle loves its scenery. 'To hear people talk,' a friend from the East assured me, 'you'd think you built Mount Rainier."

Murray Morgan, Skid Road

Variations of Labor

During our weekly childbirth
class, the peppy medical
professional tells us that today
we will be learning about labor
and the variations
of discomfort my wife
will soon experience—
the first part spent
at home watching
Netflix, the professional
suggests—
(it is important
for the partner
to remain calm)—
before the transport
to the hospital—
the admission
to triage—
the placement
of the monitor
around the patient's waist—
(it is important
for the partner
to remain calm)—
before the final push—
the contractions
intensifying—
the effaced cervix
widening—
the head

a crown—
the vulva
a valve—
(it is important
for the partner
to remain calm)—

While the professional
presses on, the phrase
variations of labor
rises in blue letters
on the big screen,
bringing to mind
not future
selfless support
but past
personal exertion,
not the voluntary
worshipful act
but mandatory
grudging depletion—
so much of the time
that we have been given
surrendered to my job
or hers,
so many of the years
spent together
devoted to other
people's needs.
I think of Jody, the woman
with cerebral palsy who
I bathed and fed and gave
medicine to with the attention
normally reserved
for a family member
towards whom one feels
an implacable debt—
who thudded tennis

balls against the walls
in a giddy fervor
of delight—
who could understand
the contempt felt
by other caregivers
for people left
in their charge—
who could understand
the love that passes
between strangers
who find themselves
confined to a room—

While the professional
pushes on, I sense
my wife tense
beside me as she takes
comprehensive notes
and am reminded
not of the woman
who I have watched grow
sure-footed and child-ready
over the past nine years
but the little girl
in elementary school
who wore glasses
coiled all the way
around her ears—
who used to flit
from classroom to playground
holding an aura
that demanded attention
beyond what a little boy
could give—
who has worked hard
to become the woman
who sustains our child.

My Uncle Was a Worker

My uncle was a worker
who would have preferred not to work

at the university he had a boss
who delighted in lording over his life's time

the time he had to be at work
was so banal a demand it went unnoticed

to have mentioned it
would have violated our country's code

at the university he collected the seeds
he found during his time on the grounds

(blackberries are an invasive species
in the part of the country where I am from)

(when your dog falls down a ravine full of blackberries
you brave the prickers to make sure he is safe)

my uncle made sure his boss's house was plentiful
with the thorns those seeds would become

(to deploy violence in response to violence
is a language most workers
would prefer not to learn)

I Was a Worker

I was a worker once.
Lent my labor to
the appetites of mass.
Like a caged animal,
my master said,
beautiful, self-contained.
Only once was I asked to sacrifice
the fingers of my left hand,
which I gave willingly
and mostly without regret.
I could follow
my master's reasoning,
was sympathetic
to her plight.
The company had
its own hunger.
We all needed
to give.

What of the other workers?
Where did they figure in?
I kept my gaze
on the task
in front of me.
I waited for
my shift
to end.

The Job at the Technology Company Cafe

The Metro bus shrieks as it turns onto Boren Avenue, *bumping and grinding* as it wraps around the corner. The phrase, more than the motion itself, reminds Andrew of his old middle school dances, and he is briefly transported back into that vast gymnasium dark, his adolescent body trying to match his movements with hers.

Andrew has never felt old before, but he feels old now. In three months, he will turn twenty-nine. Next year, he will be thirty. He has always worked in food service. He has never made more than twelve dollars an hour. The minimum wage in the city is fifteen, but there are exceptions, loopholes. At the new job, he will get thirteen-fifty even though his employer is one of the wealthiest technology companies in the world.

He stares out the Metro bus window. Street lights penetrate the early morning dark. He feels the way that he feels in dreams sometimes or the way that he moves underwater. He is not a morning person and never has been. He is not a work person, either (*he would prefer not to*, as the character in the story from AP English all of those years ago said). For a moment, he has forgotten why he accepted a job that requires of him such indecency.

He trudges up the office building steps while mist sips wetly against his cheeks. Inside, it is brighter, warmer. He flashes his badge at a security guard, then steps into an elevator, where he thumbs the button for the seventeenth floor.

Life is change, he thinks as the elevator begins to move. *Cit-*

ies are change. Isn't that what the newspapers say? He doesn't know much about other cities, but he remembers the moment when his own neighborhood began to change. The squalid brown house on the corner knocked down and two skinny towers erected in its place. The blue house across the street shoved onto stilts and literally lifted off the ground. The new Audis and Beamers, the men in suits and ties.

One summer, when he was in college at the U-Dub, he delivered a pizza to one of the new houses on his parents' block. The woman who answered the door was aloof and dismissive. And she left him a shitty tip.

Cities are change, he thinks as the elevator dings. Maybe this is true. He has only ever known one city. He has only thought of Seattle as home.

He steps out of the elevator into a silent and unfamiliar dark.

*

When Carlos called asking if he wanted a job, he told his old friend no. He already had a job working front-of-the-house at a café on Stone Way. While the situation was not ideal—his tips were shit, and the boss's son, Adam, could be a real pain in his ass—the cafe was walking distance from his apartment, the hours were flexible, and he brought home enough free food that he rarely needed to cook.

Lately, things had gotten harder. It was not only that his own rent had crept up steadily over the past few years—from $600 for the basement room when he moved in to $750 today. It was that the whole city seemed to have been turned upside down. He had seen close friends move away because of their sudden rises in rent. He had watched restaurants that he grew up in close down and disappear.

It had all happened so fast. It was like one day he was living in one city and the next he was inhabiting a totally different place.

When Carlos called, he thought at first that it was a joke. Work inside of a technology company? There was little that he could imagine that he would rather do less.

The next week of work, though, sent him over the edge. Adam chirped at him about the temperature of his lattes, and then the night barista forgot to clean the espresso machine, which made his Tuesday morning hell. When one of his regulars, a graying baby boomer who had bought a house in Wallingford back when real estate was cheap, urged him on Thursday morning to consider preparing for retirement, he decided that it was time for him to go.

He called Carlos back. He would be a cook, he thought to himself, but not only a cook. Also a spy. Something exciting for a change.

*

He walks past espresso machines and soft drinks and racks of packaged snacks to the windows through which the orange lights of South Lake Union glow alien and strange.

He remembers when the neighborhood was little more than industrial warehouses and storage facilities and car washes one drove past on their way to Seattle Center to watch the Sonics play.

He has not been to Seattle Center for years. The Sonics are gone.

"Andrew," he hears from behind him and turns.

The kitchen manager, Jose, hustles towards him with a smile on his face.

"You find it okay?" he asks, sticking out a fleshy hand.

"Found it fine," Andrew says, doesn't mention the car wash that used to be next door. He follows him through the café to the kitchen and then the narrow break room behind it. Jose hands him a white chef's coat and a black chef's cap and the key to a locker where he can store his things. He stuffs his backpack into the locker, slings the coat over his shirt. He likes the way the uniform looks. It has a clean, white, almost martial feel.

He accompanies Jose back out to the kitchen, where the manager hefts a bag of liquid egg from the counter and pours until the frying pans are full.

"Cook them low and slow," he instructs, adjusting the induction burners. "Keep them nice and soft."

Andrew cooks them low and slow. He tries to keep them nice and soft. When one pan is finished, he dumps its contents into a metal serving dish, which he hoists into a hot box stationed in the corner above the counter.

There are four other cooks—Fernando, Maria, Lorenzo, and Jose. Mostly no one speaks. A speaker blares Spanish-language music from the counter. Otherwise the kitchen is quiet as the cooks hurry about their work.

After a few hours, they open the buffet. Where before the kitchen was peaceful, now everything is rush. All is agitation. They strain to get the first round of dishes out and then they scramble to prepare more.

It is only after the rush subsides that he stands back and observes. The tech workers look young, first of all. Some are in their early twenties, others possibly their late teens. They wear hoodies and baseball caps and backpacks and flannel shirts. They look less like invaders come to take his city by force than students gathered in a school cafeteria.

After breakfast, they close down the buffet and put on pots of soup to boil. They have thirty minutes to eat and rest and recover before they return for lunch. He follows the other cooks through the buffet line, scraping the remnants of the technology workers' breakfasts onto a plastic plate.

They cluster around an orange table in the dining room. No one speaks as they concentrate on their food.

Then the youngest of them, Lorenzo, turns to him and ask, "Hey, man. Where you from?"

Andrew looks up from his waffle, surprised. "Me? Here."

"Word? Seattle?" Lorenzo nods. "I just moved here last month."

"Oh, yeah? From where?" Andrew says.

"Wenatchee. Eastern Washington. Other side of the mountains."

"I know Wenatchee," Andrew says. "I used to play chess tournaments there when I was a kid."

"I don't know nothing about no chess tournaments." Lorenzo grins. "But I could definitely tell you where to score some bomb ass mota."

The other cooks laugh. Andrew reddens, sawing at a hashbrown patty with his fork.

When Fernando says something to Jose in Spanish, Andrew is grateful to be ignored.

After lunch, they return to the kitchen where speed racks wait for them laden with aluminum trays. At lunch, most of the food is prepared off-site, he learns, before it is packed into vans and shuttled several miles to them. At lunch, they do not really cook. They unpack, assemble, arrange, and display.

Jose assigns him and Lorenzo to the flank steaks, which have been delivered cold and gray with heavy black grill marks stamped into their sides.

"You ever work as a cook before?" Lorenzo asks him as he slaps meat onto a tray.

"I used to work in a coffee shop," Andrew says. "Espresso drinks, sandwiches. That sort of thing."

"You know how to make cappuccinos?" Lorenzo asks.

"Of course," Andrew says.

Lorenzo smiles as he shoves his tray into an oven. "You know, I never had a cappuccino until I started working here," he says. "Now I have one every day."

"They give them to you for free?" he asks.

"Sometimes," Lorenzo says. He winks. "And sometimes we don't ask."

Andrew laughs. "What about you? You ever work as a cook before?"

"Nah, man. In Wenatchee, I used to work in the fields. I've been doing that since I was a little kid. Those bins are hella heavy, though, man. This shit is hella easy compared to that."

"Word," Andrew says, trying to imagine pulling apples from trees. "You still have family over there?"

"Oh, yeah. My mom, my dad, two little sisters, an older brother. A couple of aunts and uncles, too. My little cousin came to Seattle with me. You should come kick it with us, man. All we do is blaze and chill."

"For sure," Andrew says, jamming a tray into the oven. He likes the kid's energy. He seems familiar to him somehow—like someone who he used to know long ago.

*

A week goes by, and then another. He likes the early morning hours the best. Staring down into the pans, he forgets about himself and the city and the tech workers and focuses on the spatula, the frying pan, and those shimmering yellow pools.

It is harder when he has to face the tech workers, when he watched them fill their plates. Do they understand the harm that they are causing? he wonders. Do they know but not care?

He looks forwards to the time that he spends with the cooks in the cafeteria, when they gossip and eat and share stories about their lives. One afternoon, Jose tells him about growing up on a farm in southern Mexico where they had nothing to eat except for corn and a little egg. Lorenzo tells him about how his dad was deported so he had to pay thousands of dollars to get back across the border to see his family. Maria tells him about her brother who is locked up in Texas for trying to smuggle in drugs.

Andrew is surprised by how openly they cast their stories

into the air. In one way, they mean to test him. But in another, he thinks, they merely want to share.

*

He has been working in the cafe for two months when he and Lorenzo prepare a dish of steamed broccoli with oyster sauce. They unwrap the trays, transfer the broccoli onto serving dishes, and drizzle oyster sauce over the top. They gather serving utensils and set the dishes onto the buffet.

"Hey," one of the tech workers says as they are turning to leave. "The sign says, 'oyster sauce on the side.'"

They look at the tag. It does, indeed, say oyster sauce on the side.

"Next time the sign says, 'oyster sauce on the side'? *Put it on the side!*"

He stalks off.

Lorenzo looks at Andrew. Andrew looks back at Lorenzo, who turns to fling his finger at the man's fleeing back.

Their eyes dance with laughter even as their mouths remain still.

*

The next morning, Lorenzo is gone. It takes until lunch for Andrew to find out what has happened.

"They fire him," Jose says, shrugging as he breaks up a biscuit with his fingers.

"They *fired* him?" Andrew looks around the table. "Just like that?"

"Just like that," Jose agrees, pressing bread into his mouth.

"That's ridiculous," Andrew says.

"Le dije," Maria says, pointing with her fork. "Le dije a el que tenga cuidado con esos ricos idiotas."

The others nod.

"What'd she say?" Andrew asks.

"She told him to be careful," whispers Jose, "with all these rich idiots."

"We should do something," Andrew says.

"It's okay." Jose stirs his yogurt with his spoon. "He'll find another job."

"It's not right," Andrew says, tossing his fork onto his tray.

*

He plods past half-finished office buildings and construction cones and hulking orange cranes. Mist nips at his cheeks while he bows his head against the wind.

It was silly to think of himself as a spy, he thinks, trudging up the office building steps. He has no one to report back to. There is no authority who determines right and wrong. He is only a cook—someone whose only power is over the food.

Inside, he turns the induction burners to high. He pours until the frying pans are full. He cooks the eggs quickly, does not worry about keeping them nice and soft.

When the first batches are finished, he dumps the eggs into serving dishes and adds salt and little pepper, then shoves the dishes into the hot box in the corner above the counter.

When he returns the can of black pepper to the shelf, he notices a container of white pepper beside it. He has an idea.

He pulls the dishes back out from the warmer. He peels back the plastic wrap.

He adds one pinch, two pinches, three pinches, five.

For my neighborhood, he thinks as he pours. For my city. For Lorenzo. For me.

To the North Seattle NIMBY with Whom Last Week I Shared Garlic Prawns

You want more police, you said, more patrols,
all of the Aurora crap pushed away, to some other
neighborhood, some other place, someone else's
problem now, another community's fate.
Those people don't want help, anyway.
They want to snort powder in the back seats
of cars, to break into decent people's homes,
to make my mom afraid.
Our system is capitalism and democracy
which means that people will be poor.
Just keep them the hell away.

In the poem that I have been trying
to write you, I tell you about the hole
in my car where the radio used to be,
how it was taken two days before
we shared garlic prawns
at the Thai restaurant on Eastlake.
Everything civil, our disagreements peaceful,
all of us equal
so long as our bank accounts
were sturdy enough to sustain
cocktails and Pad Thai and beef salad
alongside talk of the homeless and criminal justice
and the mayor and your lawn.
You see?
I have been trying to write a poem
but all I can come up with

are banal thoughts
and prosaic observations.

In the poem that I have been trying
to write you, I tell you about the hole
in my car where the radio used to be,
how each morning I peer down
into cords and wires and Styrofoam.
How the absence regards me
like a wound, like a rupture
between the way I live now
and the experience that
used to belong to me.
I tell you about the thief
who I never saw but now sense,
how he was a small man
who was a little ashamed
while he detached the wires
causing the minimum
amount of damage.
I tell you about the pity
that he felt for me
and the lack of peace
he held in himself.
I tell you about his sadness
and fragility and fear.

In the poem that I write you,
I tell you the police
will not help you.
Tell you the prawns
will not help you.
Tell you playing civil
or socialized or familial
will not help you.
I tell you that
you will die.

My Neighborhood

In my neighborhood
there is no place to sit
unless you count the porches
since it is mostly houses here
but I am tired of clumped leaves
and empty streets, the women in scrubs
smoking, the men dragging firewood
from where to where I never ask
although we sometimes wave.
So today I have decided to walk
through the parts of my neighborhood
that I have not gotten to know
simply because I have not bothered
to walk two blocks in two years
where the houses hug the highway—
so many consciousnesses confined to cars
when I have access only to mine—
my neighborhood, my mind.
I walk past a pile of plastic
shards, its origin unclear,
a backyard greenhouse
raising who knows what,
a fence dividing corner houses
from a playground
of industrial machinery.
A man studies me
from one of the porches
with indifference or suspicion.
I wave my tea at him and carry on.
On the next block, I sit down

near a sign that reads, "STOP."
A car speeds past me
without a thought.
I wonder if I look foolish
sitting here on the ground
with a ceramic mug of tea
searching for an indication of this place
warming to me
or a warning I belong.

To the Woman Who Thought That I Was Barstaff at My Brother's Engagement Party

I, too, mistake myself for a bartender
from time to time.
While walking through an art gallery, for instance,
or a private residence like this one,
I often think to myself, that fellow there,
he looks like he could use a drink.
White Russian or Moscow Mule?
Pinot Noir or Pinot Gris?
It is one of my secret talents, actually,
divining the beverage preferences
of imperfect strangers.
I am not a professional,
I am a savant
posing as a layman—
an appreciator of art, say,
or the groom's older brother.
But you, dear woman,
saw right through me.
I thought that I was hidden
but I was recognizable
by my face.

The Morning Tournament

The blinds had gone up four times when the white guy with the mutton chops raised, the Vietnamese dude re-popped, and Jack, who held the ten eight of hearts—a hand that he would have liked to play, don't get him wrong, would have almost certainly played it if not for the re-raise—slumped his cards towards the muck. And then he would have flopped a flush. Not only that but four cards to a straight flush. He would have cleaned up, especially after Mutton Chops flopped middle set and the Vietnamese Dude moved all-in with a higher flush draw that never came.

It was deeply painful for Jack to imagine what might have been.

*

In the tournament he finished fourth. The top five spots paid, so technically he was in the money, but the prize wasn't much—thirty-five dollars on top of the forty he paid to buy in, little better than community center wages for his four hours of work. He laid his driver's license down on the poker table to let the manager take down his contact information so that he could get paid. He watched the man write down his mother's address, the number currently accurate, a source of his continuing shame.

He folded the twenties into his pocket, left five on the table for the dealer, and headed for the door. It was twelve-thirty in the afternoon and he had nowhere he needed to be.

*

He cruised back down Aurora Avenue past fast food restaurants and pay-by-the-hour motels and gas stations, all of the usual junk that he tended to tune out on his way up to the casino, when the imminent commencement of the game drew his attention away from the grimy highway that connected the leafy neighborhood where he lived to the tawdry expanse of asphalt where he spent most mornings. The ride back, though, was different, especially if he lost. Then he saw the filth with clarity, with feelings, even, of identity—as though he was part of the ugliness he passed through, as though it had begun to infect him. And while he had not lost money today, the thirty-five he earned did not feel like much of a victory either, not with first place paying five hundred and him trying to put together a bankroll.

He was tired of the morning tournament. Tired of the greasy breakfasts and flimsy, insubstantial chips. For months he pored over strategy guides in Barnes and Noble cafes, sipping mug after mug of milky coffee while scribbling notes in his sketchpad. He had watched countless World Series of Poker broadcasts on his mother's TV, paying special attention to the diminutive, sharp-witted Canadian who people in casinos sometimes said that he looked like. And he had played in dozens of morning tournaments, competing against a rotating cast of college students, degenerate gamblers, and middle-aged former strippers who seemed to have no conception of sophisticated poker strategy as described in Barry Greenstein's Ace on the River or Doyle Brunson's Supersystem. He had paid his dues.

He was ready to play in games where real money was at stake, the kind of money that would allow him to move out of his parents' place and into one of the new apartment buildings that ringed the Northgate Mall. The kind of games that would establish him as a player in the professional poker world.

There were no games like that on Aurora Avenue. To find those, he had to travel north to Tulalip or south to Muckelshoot, the Indian reservations where no-limit cash games were legal unlike in the rest of Washington state. The last time that he had gone to Tulalip, he brought four of the six hundred dollars he had to his name, played so tight and skittish that he barely stood a chance.

He needed a bankroll to sit in those games, he knew now. A couple of thousand, at least.

*

After he exited Aurora, he rounded the lake behind a gray-haired woman in a Volvo who was barely pushing thirty. He had turned down the scrambled eggs and hashbrowns that came with his tournament entry and had his mind set on a feta cheese omelet from the Continental Café.

When was the last time he had been to the Continental? he wondered, passing the drycleaner where his dad used to have his business suits pressed. Probably a year, at least. He hadn't been there since the funeral.

He passed the old high school and baseball field where he spent most afternoons after school. His dad used to hit him groundballs on the infield, hard chops into the hole for hours, one after the other. He thought about the omelet—salty, delicious feta oozing out the sides. The plate would run him fifteen dollars with tax and tip—nearly half his morning's earnings and about ten percent of his current net worth as a whole—but it would be worth it. A guy had to eat.

*

"Coffee?" the waitress asked, peering at him through low-slung bangs.

He nodded and slid his brown cup forward. She was pretty, unlike the woman who served him coffee at the tournament. This waitress had dark brown hair pulled back into a ponytail, a sweet, simply made up face. He looked down at the table while she poured.

"Anything to eat?" she asked.

"Feta cheese omelet. With a side of Greek fries."

"Good choice," she said, flashing him a grin.

His mind returned to more urgent things. He figured that he had two ways of getting the money for a bankroll together, neither of which seemed good. He could either go back to his old job working the front desk at the community center or he could call Tommy and ask him if his brother could put him to work as a driver. Tommy made more in a day delivering weed to his brother's customers around the city than Jack used to make in a week checking out basketballs and badminton rackets to teens. The trouble with that idea was that the last time he had seen his friend, he had not looked good. His build was still trim, the way it had always been, but his face was pale and puffy as though it had independently acquired weight.

Neither option sounded good. If only he could have beaten the morning tournament for the money, the way the books said. But he had not been able to beat the morning tournament— not with regularity, anyway. The stacks the players started with were too small. The blinds moved up too fast. The structure rewarded reckless play, making the game a gamble little better than blackjack.

He was startled from his thoughts by the sound of his food arriving with a thud. He tried to catch the waitress's eye, but her back was already turned.

He forked eggs to his mouth and chewed. He decided that he would give Tommy a call.

*

"The poker gig's not working out for you?" Tommy asked, piloting them past doggie daycares, French restaurants, and fancy salons. The music in the Acura was so loud—big pimpin', spendin' cheese—that the windows around them shook.

"It's going all right," Jack said. "Just not as profitable as I thought it was going to be. That's all."

"You used to beat my ass all the time in high school," Tommy said. "For whatever that's worth."

"Not much," Jack said, laughing in spite of himself. "Where we going, anyway?"

"This little pizza spot over here." Tommy gestured with his fist. "Best calzone in the city, bar none. The mozzarella comes straight from Italy."

He pulled off the main drag into a narrow alley and stopped behind a row of dumpsters. A few minutes later, a guy wearing a white apron jogged out from one of the buildings. He climbed in behind Jack.

"What up, playa?" Tommy said, reaching back across the seat.

"Chillin', brother man," the guy said.

"What you holding today, brother?" Tommy asked.

"It's called 'The New York.'" The guy handed a brown paper bag over the seat. "Olives, mushrooms, and pepperoni, and three kinds of cheese. You're going to love it."

"No doubt," Tommy said, flipping the bag onto Jack's lap. "I always love it." He reached over him to release the glove compartment and removed a tightly rolled plastic baggie from inside.

"Much appreciated," the guy said.

"Anytime," Tommy said.

They slapped hands lightly before the guy got out of the car.

He and Tommy drove north on Queen Anne towards Aurora, the music so loud again that it was hard for him to think. He preferred music that helped him to feel calm, that he could listen to at the table while he was waiting for other players to knock each other out. That was a lesson he learned from the morning tournament—poker was a contest of endurance often more than anything else.

"This calzone is unfucking real," Tommy was saying. "Best in the motherfucking city."

"All right, all right," Jack said, reaching into the bag. It was surprisingly good—salty and chewy with the perfect proportion of meat to mozzarella.

"Good, right?" Tommy asked anxiously.

"Pretty fucking good," Jack confessed, reaching for another piece.

"What'd I say?" Tommy said, wriggling his shoulders back and forth. "Perks of the muthafuckin' job!"

"Speaking of which," Jack said, eying him. "Did you ever talk with your brother?"

Tommy nodded, keeping his eyes on the road. "I did ask him. Yesterday. After you called. Unfortunately, he doesn't seem to have much work in the city right now. He does sometimes need guys to go down to Portland, though. Pick up one thing, drop another thing off. Guys make a lot of money that way."

"Pick up what?" Jack asked. "Drop what off?"

"Nah," Tommy said, shaking his head. "You don't ask. You don't look. Plausible deniability that way."

"Sounds risky," Jack said.

Tommy nodded. "Riskier than what I do, for sure. But the reward's higher, too. Fifteen hundred or two thousand just for the one trip."

"Two thousand?" Jack repeated.

Tommy shrugged. "You can think about it. It doesn't have to be you."

Jack looked at his friend. "What if I want it to be?"

*

A few weeks later, on the express lanes in north Seattle, he brought a borrowed Corolla up to seventy before thinking better of it. Several years ago, on another trip to Portland, he had picked up a speeding ticket near Olympia. Later, he learned that the town (Chehalis, he remembered it was called) was a notorious speed trap, that the small town cops hid beside the highway in wait.

He decided to lower the speed to sixty once he reached Olympia.

In the meantime, he would keep the engine steady at sixty-five, contenting himself with the compromise of a minor risk.

He passed Federal Way and then Auburn, the sedan quiet as it sped over the slick highway, the only sound made by windshield wipers sweeping away rain.

He tried to remember the last time that he had been to Portland. It must have been three or four years ago now, when he was back from college for winter break. He and Tommy had gone down on a lark—they stayed in a hostel in the southeast, went drinking in bars on Hawthorne, finished the night in a strip club that unexpectedly served steaks. He pitied Tommy then, he remembered, as much as he would have hated to admit it. His friend lived at home with his parents, took a few classes at Central, still sold weed to his high school friends.

He passed Tacoma with the depressing white dome, then Lakewood, where all the cops had been shot. Tommy had been the one who was in trouble then. Tommy was the one for whom the future looked bleak.

He settled deeper into his memory. As a kid, he had gone down a couple times with his dad. They shopped for books at Powell's, gorged on Simpson's-themed donuts at Voodoo, went to the Rose Garden to watch the Trail Blazers play. It was hard to believe that a whole year had passed. It still did not seem real.

He approached the dingy white capitol building of Olympia and eased his foot from the gas. Only thirty miles until Chehalis. Still more than two hours until he reached Portland.

The speedometer plunged towards safety. A soaring feeling filled his chest.

No, fuck that, he thought, swerving his foot back onto the gas.

The little car went.

Chehalis.

Toledo.

Castle Rock.

Longview.

No cops that he could see.

He pressed on.

He boarded the bridge that divided Vancouver and Portland and one state from the other. The Columbia River churned to both sides of him, dull, gray, and frenzied-looking.

He imagined yanking the wheel to the side. The Corolla plowing through guard rail. The release he would feel as he began his final descent.

He gripped the steering wheel with both hands.

C'mon, man. Keep it the fuck together.

He pressed on.

He passed the hulk of a closed-down gas station. A Popeye's Fried Chicken. Houses with bars over their windows. Other with boards nailed over their doors.

He imagined two thousand dollars in crisp hundred-dollar bills.

He pressed on.

The motel was where it was supposed to be. So was the Mexican grocery store. He was supposed to leave the car at the motel and spend at least thirty minutes inside the market. A shoebox on the passenger seat was the signal that the exchange had been made.

He parked and shut off the engine. His hands were trembling. He felt cold.

There was still time to change his mind. He hadn't done anything yet.

He imagined the morning tournament. Greasy, flavorless

hashbrowns. Cheap, meaningless chips.

He pulled his hood over his head and got out of the car.

He ducked past a scowling cashier at the front and slumped down an aisle stocked with dried beans and rice and chili peppers. In the back of the store, a teenaged girl slumped behind the counter staring at her phone. Displayed behind her were pictures of the different menu items—sopes, tacos, tortas, quesadillas.

"Three tacos," he said to her. "And a side of rice and beans."

"What kind do you want?" she asked, still staring at her phone.

"Carnitas," he said louder.

"Anything to drink?" She was looking at him now.

"A Coke."

"Mexican or regular?"

"Mexican," he said.

He paid for the food with cash. He took a seat at one of the plastic tables. His phone said it was 2:18. He would wait until 2:50 to go back to the car.

He drank the Mexican Coke. It really was better than the American—sweeter, not as fake.

He thought about how he normally ordered carnitas in Mexican restaurants. When he was little, he used to go with his dad to a place on Lake City Way after baseball games sometimes. His dad would order carnitas and practice Spanish with the waitresses. Jack would order cocas en bolsas—bottles of Coke poured into clear plastic bags.

What would his dad think, Jack wondered, about what he was doing now? His father had always seemed to like that Jack played poker. He thought that it was adventurous, even brave. It had been his father who encouraged him to study the game like a profession. If you like it so much, he said, treat it like work. Of course, gambling was one thing. Transporting drugs (or whatever it was) across state lines was quite another.

The girl brought his tacos on a paper plate. He tried to catch her eye, but her back was already turned. He squeezed lime over the first taco, nestled radish into the meat. For a moment he could not think. Everything in his mind was given over to the food.

He drank more of the Coke to clear his head. He wondered what his mom would think, wondered whether she thought about him at all. After his dad died, he thought grief might bring them closer together. Instead, the gulf between them had, if anything, grown.

Anyway, it didn't matter what either of them thought. It was his own decision. It was his call to make.

*

When he opened the door, the shoebox was on the passenger seat, the cardboard darkened and spattered by rain. He set it down on the floor, resisting the urge to look inside.

He would stay under the speed limit on the way back, he decided as he started the engine. He had no reason to tempt fate now. He was almost there.

Approaching Chehalis, he noticed a cop parked on the shoulder, his boxy black speedgun pointed at northbound cars.

He checked the rearview mirror. The cop hadn't budged.

He pressed on.

The traffic slowed in downtown Seattle. The dark gray buildings resembled towering stacks of chips. This time tomorrow, he thought, licking his dry lips, he would be at Tulalip a steak on one side of him and a stack of clay chips on the other.

He checked his phone. It was almost seven. At home, his mom would be boiling water for pasta or simmering a pot of soup. The evening tournament on Aurora would just be getting off the ground.

Then he thought of the Continental. Maybe the pretty waitress would be there.

"Anything to drink?" a waitress asked, but it was a different woman. She barely looked at him while she set down a napkin and knife and fork.

He slid his coffee cup forward. Outside, on the sidewalk, a man was sprawled on the ground with an open guitar case in front of him. What a bum, Jack though. Lazy beyond belief.

"Anything besides coffee?" his waitress asked, setting the pot of coffee on the counter behind her.

"A feta cheese omelet," Jack said without looking at her. "And a side of Greek fries."

"Sounds good," the waitress said.

"Hold on," Jack said. "And chocolate milk."

"Sure thing," the waitress said.

"And a side of regular fries," he said.

"You mean instead of the Greek?"

"No. In addition to the Greek."

"Okay."

"And a piece of baklava. No, make it two."

She looked down at him. Her eyes were luminous, concerned.

"I just need to eat." He blinked back tears. "I promise. Then I'll be fine."

Not a Doctor

My uncle was not
the doctor
with voluminous hair
who told me
when I was young
that it was important
never to make
too much money

but he could have been
 a doctor
or prophet
if he had more
confidence or if all his hair
hadn't fallen out when
he was young
or if he wasn't so suspicious
of specialized work.

Oh, uncle, I'll miss our conversations
about capitalism and systemized
greed, the feta cheese omelets
from the corner diner
garnished with Greek fries
and sorrow, tooling around
in your terrible truck
half-drunk
on disappointment.

Variations of Labor/ 37

I have heard
that our economic system
rewards intelligence
and hard work.
I have also heard
that the living
do not haunt the living
with the same urgency
as do the dead.
I know now that neither
of these things
are true.

The Laugh

His hands
scraping together
like sticks
in a last-ditch effort
to make
the mouth
catch fire

When My Parents Were Hippopotamuses

When my parents were hippopotamuses
they wore tiny, immaculate strawberries
on their fingers like rings.
They didn't have to taste them.
They knew that they were extraordinary.
The president at that time was a reporter
from Long Island who supported reparations
for militant minorities but also could trace
the contours of white people's shame.
Most people used drugs but the kind
that caused them to broach indescribable
universes, not berate their friends
into taking more personal responsibility.
The public buses were funded by vast
rich people who believed that competition
would convert communities into repositories
of good will.
Their thinking was wrong
but people forgave them
because the busses were free.
Herbal tea solved
most health problems.
The rest were addressed by benevolent
biker gangs who rode from town to town
consoling the distraught and unwell.
My parents lived on a farm
in a saltwater pool where they ate
all the fish they could catch
with their pink hippopotamus mouths.

Mostly they were silent
but sometimes they spoke
the clearest songs
you can imagine.

David's Friend

David closed the document, stood up from his desk, and walked to the window. Outside, on the street, pedestrians scurried through light rain. He thought about going out for a short Americano with steamed soy milk from Vivaldi's, but he had already drank two coffees today (one from the pot Patricia made, then a second from the drive-through near the entrance to the freeway) and it was not yet ten.

Three months ago, his friend Matthew was walking down Broadway with a morning paper in one hand and cappuccino in the other (he had been sanguine that morning, according to his regular barista, bantering with strangers about baseball while scattering croissant crumbs across the counter) when he staggered, dropped his paper, and fell to the pavement to stay.

It had not been the first time that David lost someone close. His own father died a decade ago from complications related to Parkinson's disease and Patricia's mother succumbed to ovarian cancer only the year before last. But those deaths had been prefaced in ways that Matthew's was not. The hospital visits and hotel rooms, the brief handshakes with doctors and banal exchanges with nurses, even the bad daytime television helped cushion the blow. He had been allowed time in those instances to arrange his feelings into order.

With Matthew, he had been allowed nothing.

*

"More beets, dear?" Patricia asked that night at dinner as she heaped another helping of arugula onto her plate.

"Still working on these." He gestured to his plate as he lifted his glass of Orvieto to his lips.

He had stopped at Ernie's on his way home from work, his go-to place near Alki Beach. The shop was filled with tasteful lighting, congenial employees, and difficult-to-find Italian whites. He had been going to Ernie's for so long that the owner greeted him by name.

There had been a time when he had taken real pleasure in that recognition. He felt comforted by it, somehow. Recently, however, he found himself cutting their conversations short. The man was not his friend.

"How's the book coming?" Patricia asked, refilling her water glass.

He studied his wine. She didn't mean book. She meant manual. She meant reference guide. He brought the glass to his nose and sniffed. Hints of almond, apple, possibly cherry. He drank, swallowing carefully.

"I said, how's the book coming, David," she repeated.

He set the glass back on the table. "Oh, you know. Standard health-nut boilerplate. Whole grains are good for you. So, too, fruit." He snorted. "Who said to make it new? Some poet, wasn't it? Somebody dead?"

"Don't be morbid, David." She halved a beet with her fork, juice squirting out the sides. "Something about it must be new. Or what's the point of writing it? Publishing it, for that matter?"

He grinned, revealing wine-darkened teeth. "What's the point, indeed?"

*

In the first days after Matthew's death, his widow hosted a series of potlucks in their prominent Montlake home. David lived more than twenty minutes away, yet he managed to attend every one.

He was surprised to discover that he knew only a few of

Matthew's other friends. They were a bohemian bunch, clad in earrings, goatees, and attractively disheveled hair, and he was surprised, too, to learn that these were the people with whom Matthew had chosen to surround himself. Dressed in muted-tone sweaters and slacks, his own graying hair clipped close to his head, he listened in diffident silence to the guests honor their departed friend. In speeches at once stagy and intimate, they bemoaned the brevity of life, the democracy of death, and the especially inordinate tragedy of Matthew's premature passing. After they finished speaking, the yard sang with the pounding of open palms.

But David was unmoved. These were the things that people usually said, he thought, when confronted with an unfathomable event, and while they were not untrue exactly, they were hardly adequate, either, to encompass the enormity of the emotion at hand. Perhaps that was why the speakers looked a little sheepish when they were finished.

Still, he attended the potlucks. He went with an involuntary faithfulness, standing in a corner of the room with a plastic cup of white wine and paper plate of pasta salad, face contorted into a recognizable expression of grief. In this way he was able to keep his emotions at bay.

It had been Matthew's family who threatened to undo him. Their faces were so naked in those early days, as though a crucial, protective layer had been stripped away to reveal the full force of their suffering beneath. He had not been able to console the widow or her children. For he, too, needed to be consoled.

*

He opened the manuscript document, took a sip of his coffee, and promptly turned off his computer. He rubbed his beard with both hands and leaned back in his chair.

For the better part of thirty years David had been correcting writers' misspellings, amending their tense inconsistencies, and rectifying their syntactical errors. He thought of himself as a kind of launderer, someone who gathered up dirty copy and sent it back clean.

There was a time, however, when he put sentences together himself. First, he had tried his hand at fiction. Later, he dabbled in screenplays. Then he stopped writing altogether. He was afraid of making a mistake, he thought now, not of grammar, but of temperament, of human sensibility. He was afraid that he would reveal himself to be a fool.

Courage, he thought, looking down at the street. That had been the quality that so attracted him to his friend, kept him looking forward to their lunches and impromptu morning espressos. Alive, Matthew glittered against the encroaching blandness of David's life, brilliant, even obscene.

And what, he wondered, had his friend thought of him? When they first met, Matthew was a young attorney in the county prosecutor's office while David edited freelance for magazines and wrote screenplays on the side. There had been a sense that they were going places.

Of course, Matthew had.

*

David almost never went to Pike Place Market. It was the sort of place that he liked to bring his friends visiting from out of town, then abandoned the rest of the year for Trader Joe's or QFC. It was strange one morning to find himself wandering the linoleum floors in bleary search of a cup of coffee.

Even stranger still was the sight of Matthew's widow, who he spotted near the fruit stands at the front entrance of the market, her head bowed slightly as though praying to the fruit.

He thought about ducking across the alley into the Italian specialty store to hide out among olives and artichoke hearts and logs of aged salami. But it was too late.

"David," she called, waving. "David!"

He nodded, starting towards her. "I thought that might be you."

They embraced in the street. Her raincoat was clammy against his hands.

"How are you, David?" She held his shoulders. "It's been ages and ages."

"It's been far too long," he agreed, shifting feet. "More importantly, how are you and the kids doing?"

She smiled, which only served to underscore her sadness. "The kids are fine, I think. Lauren's staying on at Whitman over the break to work with a professor."

"That's wonderful," he said, looking past her. On the corner, a man was selling newspapers. He had left his own copy at home that morning, he realized. He would have to buy another.

"Tommy's still living at home," the widow was saying. "Honestly, I don't know what I would do without him."

A homeless man, tattooed and filthy-looking, lurched near them. David took the widow by the arm, guiding her towards a donut stand, where two teenagers were wolfing pastries out of a brown paper bag. They licked their fingers and plunged them back in.

"We should have dinner," the widow was saying. "You, me, and Patricia. I've been looking for an excuse to cook."

"Absolutely," he said. "Let's set something up."

"It would be great to see you and Patricia again."

"Of course. I'll send out an email. We'll get a date on the calendar."

"David?" she asked.

"Yes?"

"Would you like to have a cup of coffee with me? That bakery across the alley makes the most wonderful espresso."

"Of course," he said, against his will.

*

David remembered when it was difficult to find an espresso drink in Seattle. He and Matthew used to seek out hole-in-the-wall Italian groceries in Rainier Valley and upscale specialty shops in Pioneer Square. Now you could find a mediocre latte on every block.

The cappuccino was good—the espresso complex, the milk perfectly frothed. He fiddled with the foam while his friend's widow complain. She complained about her colleagues at work; about the administrators in charge of Matthew's life insurance; about Republican politicians in Congress; about the national economy. He listened until he could listen no more. Then he focused on her forehead, the peculiar length and gleam of it. If he looked in a certain way, he was reminded of the donuts in the market. He imagined dusting the crevices with handfuls of powdered sugar.

"And you, David?" she said finally. "You've hardly said anything about yourself."

He set the cappuccino on its saucer. "The same old for me," he said. "Patricia's working hard at the library. I'm currently editing a sort of manuscript."

"A manuscript, David?" She leaned closer. "What kind of book is it?"

"Not a book," he said, gripping the cup. "More of a nutritional guide. What to eat and avoid and so on. I force myself to work on it during the mornings. When I try to read that stuff at night, my head sprints straight for the pillow."

He laughed. It was barely a burp, at first, but it ballooned, burgeoning into a high, manic, nearly uncontrollable thing.

When he could see again, the widow was scrutinizing him closely.

"I'm sorry, David," she said, "that you're not happy with your work."

*

Not happy with my work? David thought later that afternoon, staring into his computer screen. He had not been happy with his work for fifteen years. It never stopped him before.

But in fact that was what Matthew's death had felt like—a

termination, a kind of ending, of his previous life. His usual habits and routines had gone on for so long that they almost seemed permanent. Nothing was permanent, he understood now in a way that he had not quite before. Not Matthew, not Patricia, certainly not him.

The knowledge was toxic. He turned away from the window. It should be sealed under a mountain where nobody lived.

*

He stopped at Ezell's on his way home from work. It was his favorite chicken in the city, a treat that Patricia allowed him only once per month.

He drove home through irritating rain. He had barely set his bag down on the floor before he pulled a breast from the Styrofoam and jabbing it to his mouth. It was perfect—still warm and moist with a hard, crunchy crust.

"How was work, dear?" his wife asked from behind him, pecking him on the head.

"It was fine," he said, reaching for a wing before finishing the breast, wanting to keep up the continuity of sensation.

"How's the book coming along?" she asked, opening the container of cornbread.

"For Christ sake!" he exclaimed, dropping the wing on the counter.

"What is it, David?" she cried.

"How many times have I told you? It's not a fucking book." He took a deep breath. "Look, you want to know about the damned nutritional guide so bad, I'll tell you. It says that five small meals a day are better for you than three. Brown rice is preferable to white. And do you have any idea—any real conception—how long it takes the average adult human being to digest a half a pound of red meat?"

She shook her head slowly.

"Days," he said, retrieving the wing from the counter. "Something like three."

He bit down on bone but kept chewing, the smaller animal's skeleton submitting easily to his.

"And don't get me started on fried foods," he put in. He felt the urge to laugh again—to surrender to the same manic force that had seized him with the widow. "Make sure that you avoid those at all costs."

*

The next month, he turned fifty-seven. Patricia suggested that they throw a party, a dinner that would bring together all of his friends. He would have preferred to spend a quiet night at home—dinner, a movie, maybe scotch, sex—but his wife would not be deterred.

Patricia created the guest list, mailed out the invitations, and secured the restaurant reservation. All that is left for him to do was show up, which he did about a half an hour ahead of time.

A waiter led him to the back room where hors d'oeuvres had been laid out on silver trays. There were mushrooms stuffed with pesto, several varieties of olive, plastic cups of sautéed squid. Wine bottles on one of the tables like military officers at attention. He went over to release one.

He had nearly finished it before the first guest arrived.

*

All of these people here for me, David thought. All of them come for me.

In truth, he hardly recognized them. Their hair had gone gray or bi-colored. Their bodies were plump and frail. They looked like caricatures of his old friends, the people with whom he has spent his formational Seattle years.

At his table, two men were discussing a law that affected nightclubs, homeless people, levels of sound. He was having trouble following the conversation. He wasn't sure why he should care.

Matthew would have cared, he thought, swirling his wine. Matthew would have had something interesting to say—something either to support or else to strenuously oppose. The effect would have been exchange, debate, the flow of ideas.

With people like these there was nothing very forceful going on. Just the polite rehashing of news and secondhand information passed along.

Across the room, he spotted her—the widow is standing near the table of hors d'oeuvres. Her hair was wet, her face arranged in an anxious expression.

He didn't invite her, he thought, clutching his glass. Then again, he hadn't invited anybody. Patricia must have put her on the list. After the party, he would speak with her.

"Speak with who?" one man asked.

"Are you all right?" asked the other.

"Fuck the both of you," he said as he rose from his chair.

Nearly three months had passed since he saw her in the market. He had not responded to her email. He had neglected to call her back. Now here she was in front of him close enough to touch.

"David!" She reached out. "Happy birthday!"

He clutched her and released. "I didn't expect to see you here. I didn't know you that you'd been invited."

She recoiled as though he had raised his fist. "Of course I was invited, David! Patricia sent me a card."

He stepped past her to the refreshments. "I just meant that it's been a long time. That's all."

"I sent e-mails. You never wrote me back."

He uncorked a bottle and tipped it towards his glass.

"I left phone messages," she said. "You never called."

He dribbled a little red on the tablecloth as he finished his pour. He scooted a bottle over the stain.

"What happened, David?" she said. "You and Matthew were so close once. Why didn't you write me back?"

"Because," he said, turning around to face her, "you weren't my friend."

*

They were supposed to take Patricia's car home and leave his where it was parked, but as he came out from the restaurant onto the street he realized that he was alone. The widow's face returned—her injury and surprise. Why had he said that to her? He should have apologized, tried to patch things up. The woman had been through enough.

But not only her, he thought, looking out at the water. Not the window alone. All of Matthew's friends suffered. The grief did not only belong to her.

"David!" he heard someone yell. He whirled, nearly fell.

"There you are," his wife said, starting towards him.

They embraced in the street, her sweater warm against his hands.

"Did you have a good time?" she asked, rubbing his back.

"Wonderful," he said.

"It was a nice party, wasn't it?" she said.

"A great party," he said. "You were right to want to have it."

She beamed and kissed his cheek. "Will you walk down to the water with me?"

He nodded and allowed himself to be led.

They ambled past parked cars and shrubbery towards a beach of empty sand. The Puget Sound shimmered in the distance. It was so dark and endless, he thought, a vast, inscrutable maw.

"There are so many people in this city who care about you, David," she said. She turned to him. "You know that, don't you? You have so many friends."

He leaned down and kissed her mouth. "What if I only care about you?"

Tears budded at the edges of her eyes.

His friend, he thought. His friend. He had loved him all along.

Relief

Certain months
the mind goes.
It can be hard
to latch on
to anything,
to command
or compel.
Meanwhile, the body
wanders, performs,
does its daily
diligence,
angers no one,
its own anger
gone, replaced by
weightlessness, calm.
The mind says,
this is progress,
a procession
forward,
but the body
resists.
First, the stomach
begins to crimp,
then the face
shows blankness
those mornings
it bothers to look.
But the mind

isn't shook.
It says,
grow yourself
a beard.
Remember
to brush
your teeth.

Another Way of Saying Fear

The morning unfolds today
with a slowness that seems rare.
At some point, my life began
to acquire a shape and texture
that I did not anticipate.
Take the espresso cup
on the desk.
Take the beans,
the grinder,
I don't care.
A long time ago I ceased
being concerned with
other people's opinions,
a statement that is untrue,
demonstrably, yet one
I repeat most mornings.
Which is another way
of saying fear.
Fear of other people's hell,
of the eternity of self
dissolving,
of the angry, suburban
dad who I saw shouting
yesterday at the TV screen
while I watched
football in a bar.

I wanted to do to him
what I do to you at home:
wrap him up, tell him everything
was going to be alright.
Fear of what else?
My life
collapsing again
against the end
of each day.

Near Boats

At the table
near boats
with creaking
iron-wrought chairs
and glasses filled
with martini-drink
we come together
to close
some of the distance
life has wrought
since my father
fought and lost.
Like a waterfall
that never stops
time can weather
whatever closeness
manages to hang on.
Yet today we are here
with cold drinks
on a cold day
smiling
while afternoons
shorten
and fold
as though they
never were,
as though we
could start again
together,

however
improbable
that might
seem.

The Organizer

To his first day of work, the boy wore black shoes, black slacks, and a blue button-down shirt. They were only dress clothes he owned. The only ones he had thought to bring with him on the move.

The other trainees were similarly dressed. The exception was an older guy at the end of the table who wore a black tee-shirt and jeans. The boy decided that he would like him. The others he did not like. He thought them glossy, snide. He wondered why they were here.

Then a veteran organizer at the front of the room stood to face them. He wore a brown hooded sweatshirt and jeans and sported a surly expression on his face. After he introduced himself, he turned his back on them. He made brusque marks on the black chalkboard.

As the man spoke, the boy's mind skittered, leapt. He wondered if he would be bad at this job, thought, maybe, the union would provide him with a GPS.

*

Three months earlier the boy had moved to Seattle without knowing anyone at all. He spent the summer delivering pizzas and bussing tables while living with his parents at home. He saved enough money that he figured he had enough to survive for a few months in the big city while he was figuring out what to do with his life.

This was the fall of 2008. The housing crisis just hit and the wheels of the national economy were beginning to fall off. After arriving in Seattle, he applied for every job that he could find. He applied for office jobs and restaurant jobs, coffee shop jobs and valet parking jobs, telemarketing jobs and casino security guard jobs. He didn't hear a word.

While the boy waited for someone to write him back, he sat in his studio apartment and drank French-pressed coffee and smoked hand-rolled cigarettes and made himself bean and cheese quesadillas in a pan. He read articles about the financial crisis, watched movies on Netflix, jerked off to internet porn, and smoked. Once each day he sat on his apartment buildings steps and watched people trot by with espresso drinks, dry-cleaning, computer bags, takeout Thai.

It was strange the feeling of not having enough. His family had never been rich, but they always had enough. Even when he was in college he had not had to think about money much. The loans and scholarships took care of tuition. His college ID card allowed him to eat most days.

He knew what it was like to serve people. During high school, he worked in a restaurant and grocery store. Away at college, he work-studied, keeping time at swim meets and setting stages for authors and musicians. He knew intimately the degradations of low-wage work, the obliviousness and entitlement of customers, the callousness and cruelty of higher-ups.

For him, though, the money had been extra, since his parents always paid most of his bills. It was different for the people who he worked with. Many of them were older and had no college degree. Others had degrees but could find no work to apply their skills. One woman who he remembered held a doctorate in English Literature. She had written her dissertation on Ezra Pound. At the time, he had felt sorry for her, sure. But mostly he had not given her much thought. Now he was ashamed.

More than forty percent of the nation's resources were controlled by the top one percent, he read online. Thirty million people had no health insurance. Fifty million people were on food stamps.

Had it always been this way in the United States? the boy wondered. Or was this something new?

After seeing a post on Craigslist, he sent an application into the union on a whim. He was invited to interview the very next day.

*

The boy's job was to drive from house to house and ask grocery store workers to sign cards declaring support for a union election. After the union had collected enough cards, they would file them with the National Labor Relations Board. Once a majority of workers voted yes, the union would be authorized to represent them in negotiations with their employer.

That was nearly as much as the boy knew about practical aspects of union business. During the first week, he sat through a succession of presentations, each of them detailing a different aspect of the campaign. He understood the information being imparted was important, but he found it difficult to concentrate or keep the details straight.

From the beginning, he had planned on using his own experience working in grocery stores to connect with people at the doors. "Don't get lost in the weeds," one of the organizers said. He meant to keep the organizing conversations strictly canopy-level and above.

*

On his first day on the doors, the boy drove north while the clouds sputtered rain. The sky was gray. The road was gray. Even the cars were gray. How did people stand it? he wondered, reaching for the radio.

On NPR, a man whose voice he recognized but whose face he couldn't picture was talking about climate change and the threat it posed. If Americans didn't cut down on consumption soon, the man said, we would pass the point of no return.

Limousine liberal, the boy thought, spinning down the

sound. He didn't give a damn about working people.

The first house on his list was in a neighborhood where all the houses looked the same. Curb-mounted basketball hoops, paved walkways and furred welcome mats. Staunch American flags and dusty SUVs. He pulled in behind a pickup truck and knocked on the front door.

"I'm not interested," said the man who answered before the boy could introduce himself.

"I'm not selling anything, sir," he said, trying to smile. "I'm here because workers from all over the state are coming together—"

"Like I said," the man said. "I'm not interested. Now get the hell off my porch."

The boy tried to laugh as he went back down the steps. What an asshole that guy was, the boy thought. But his heart would not stop pounding until he was three blocks away.

At the second house, he found trash bags on the front porch and a couch blocking the door. He parked behind a rotten-looking sedan and walked around the side of the house, where he found a cluster of chickens scuffling around a wooden picnic table.

Beyond the chickens he saw a woman. Crouched low to the ground, she hacked at the dirt with some kind of wooden gardening tool.

"Hey, there," the boy called.

She turned, looked, seemed unsurprised.

"Is Pavel here, please?" he asked.

"Why do you want?" Her accent was Russian or eastern European.

"It's about work," he said, clasping his hands. "Workers coming together."

She ambled towards the house. The man who emerged wore

dark blue overalls and black work boots, the laces untied. He lurched across the grass pawing with one hand at his eyes.

"Pavel?" the boy asked, extending his hand.

"Who are you?" the man said in the same accent as the woman.

"I'm here," the boy said, "because workers from all over the state are coming together to form a union." He smiled. "Have you ever been part of a union before?"

"Union?" the man repeated.

"That's right," said the boy.

The man smiled. "I want to know what union can do about New World Order."

"What's that?" said the boy.

"The United Nations," the man said impatiently. "The Federal Reserve. I want to know what union can do about them."

The boy was silent while the man ranted about politicians, bankers, and the Catholic Church. After he finished, the boy offered a few theories of his own. Only by coming together with his fellow workers, he said, could they solve the problems that he described. Only by acting collectively could they make change in the world. If they joined the union they could—

"All right, all right." Pavel patted his shoulder. "Let me see the card."

At his next house, the woman invited him inside. He followed her through the kitchen to a living room where a bald man was hammering away at a video game while behind him three gazed raptly at the screen.

He thought back to his own childhood home, where video games were not allowed. He tried to imagine his own father playing them but could not. After the man put down the controller, the family turned its attention to the boy. He explained the authorization cards, the election, and everything that was at stake. Then he asked the oldest girl on the couch if she would describe her experience working at the store.

Her manager was all right, she said, but he had a temper with those he didn't like. She didn't get benefits, but she hadn't expected any. She'd keep on working there unless she found something better.

As the boy listened to the girl, he felt love bloom inside him. He found her beautiful. The whole family was.

He loved these people who had invited him into their home. He loved himself for being there when there were so many other places that he could be. He loved the union for making the experience possible.

It helped that the girl signed the card.

*

The weeks that followed were the most satisfying of the boy's young professional life. He found that he enjoyed asking workers questions and listening to them talk about their lives. He mentioned the union only sparingly. He brought up politics never.

After work, he took himself out to bars in Ballard that were walking distance from his apartment. He sat at the counter and sipped craft beer out of pint glasses and watched sports on the small-screen TVs and smiled at the pretty hipster girls. One night, one girl smiled back.

"Hey, man," she said, thudding her pint glass onto the bar beside him. "You're always sitting up here by yourself. What's your story?"

"No story," the boy said, flushing. "I'm just…winding down after work."

She took a moment to consider him. "Computer programmer?"

"Nope," he said.

"Bank teller?"

"Not that either."

"Dog catcher?"

"Union organizer," he said, a little proudly.

"Far out," she said, clinking his glass.

He doffed an imaginary cap.

"What's that mean, anyway? You organize papers in an office or something?"

"No. I drive around to people's houses and talk to them about joining the union. I organize people."

"No shit."

"Shit," he said. "How about you? What kind of work do you do?"

"I'm a piecer," she said, laughing. "I piece things together. A little of this, a little of that. The real thing I do, though, is play music."

"Oh, yeah?" he said. "In college, I played a little guitar."

"Yeah? You still play?"

"No. Not recently, anyway."

"That's a shame," she said.

"Not really. It's kind of a luxury, when you think about it. When there are so many people suffering in the world."

"Art's necessary," she said, reddening.

"You know how many people are on the streets right now?" the boy said. "Who have no health insurance? Did you know that the top one percent has more money than—"

She lifted her glass from the counter. "I don't want to talk to you anymore."

*

About three months after the boy started working for the union, he found himself driving north on Aurora Avenue towards Sugar's, a strip club he passed numerous times over the weeks. It had a blinking sign of a silhouetted dancer and an old school marquee advertising cheap ribeye steaks.

Who would eat in a place like that? he had thought as he drove past. Now he pulled sheepishly into the lot.

Neon lights peered down at him as he hurried over the asphalt. Is this a thing that people do? he wondered. Did people do this? The only time that he had ever been to a strip club was on the night the last of his high school friends turned eighteen. A girl had been nice to him that day, he remembered, rubbed his head and called him sweet. Now he wondered how much of his money she had been able to keep.

At the door, a bouncer asked for ID, which he showed. Inside, a woman asked him for the five-dollar entry fee, which he paid. She led him into the next room where a tall, topless woman was shimmying around a stage.

For some time he watched the woman do her work. Though pretty, she was not more attractive than the woman who had greeted him at the door. Why did one woman work the stage, he wondered, and the other the floor? Was it their choice? A function of their respective seniorities? He wondered how their bosses were, if they ever tried to organize.

The song became something soft, sweet. The stripper slowed, swaying towards the back of the stage. Her eyes were closed. Her mouth moved. She was singing, mouthing the words or belting them out, he could not be sure.

For a moment, he thought that recognizing her loneliness might alleviate his own. Instead, it made him ache more.

The song ended. She gathered her scattered singles and stomped off the stage.

Some time later, she appeared on the floor. The boy followed her with his eyes. Eventually they found hers.

She teetered toward him on high heels. "Hey, baby. Care for a dance?"

He gestured to seat across from him. "How about I buy you a drink first," he said.

"They don't serve drinks here, baby."

"They don't?"

"None with alcohol, anyway." She laughed. "This your first

"No," he said. "Not my first."

"You must be new to town then."

"How about you? Where you from? Originally?"

"Here, baby," she said. "Born and raised."

"What was that like?" he asked. "Growing up here, I mean?"

"You need to relax, baby." She stroked his knee. "How about that dance now? I'll give you two songs for the price of one. That's a good deal."

He felt himself begin to stiffen. He straightened in the hard chair.

"They treat you all right here?" he heard himself ask.

"Who's that, baby?"

"Your boss," he said. "Your manager. Whoever's in charge."

"Why you asking about that?"

"Because..." he stuttered. "Because I care."

She leaned close to whisper into his ear. "C'mon, baby. You know that that's not what this is all about."

*

The next morning, he drove east away from the city under a sky that pummeled his windshield with rain. Next to him on the passenger seat were a stack of worker contact sheets and directions printed out from MapQuest. The union, he had learned, did not provide organizers with GPS systems, although they were allowed to acquire their own.

He proceeded onto a series of smaller roads until he found himself in a neighborhood where there were no sidewalks or street signs. He had entered a trailer park, he realized. He had never been inside a trailer park before.

A few trailers down, he found the address that he was looking for. He pulled in behind an Oldsmobile and went to the door.

"You're from the union?" the woman who answered snarled after identified himself.

"Like I was saying, ma'am," the boy said, "I'm here because

workers from all over the state are coming together—"

"To take money out of my pocket? To pay people like you?"

"No, ma'am, coming together because—"

"You don't look like much more than a boy," she said, softening. "What's your name, son?"

"My name?" the boy repeated.

"Who are you? Why don't we start there."

He shrank back on the porch. He felt dizzy. "I don't see how that matters," he whispered. The woman's eyes—they burned right through.

"It matters plenty, son. It's the whole goddamned thing."

*

He began listening to more music while he drove. Songs that soothed him, quieted his throbbing heart.

Why had he come here? What did he want?

Staring up at evergreen-streaked skies, he realized that he didn't know.

The Grays

The grays hung over me
and were hard to puncture through,
no thoughts or divinity
to spell the shabbiness
my mind had become
accustomed to.
I filled my mouth
with cool water,
became a madman
for exercise,
reduced my carbohydrate
intake to a minimum.
On highways I passed trucks
that wanted only to crowd me
or fling water against the glass.
I stopped at gas stations
to buy corn chips that mounted
temporary arguments against
my ongoing ruin.
I stared out at grays
and peered into them.
I held them inside of me
wherever I went.
I found them as soothing
and suffocating as smoke
or any other toxifying beauty.

Apocalypse Greens

I was having a conversation
about sweet potato greens
when someone said I love you
which was strange
because I was sitting alone
at my kitchen table
with a bottle of hot sauce
boasting its freedom
from gluten which to my mind
was redundant because
who would add wheat
or barley or any other
gluten-containing contaminant
to a spicy pepper fluid
intent only on enhancing
a food's flavor profile
while at the same time
vanishing from visible
perception completely
when someone said I love you
or I saw the potential
of a person saying that
or I recognized the space
for the possibility
of that imagining
and I thought
if that reality
came to pass

the world might
cease to be.

Lenny's Rap

"Yo, can I get a dub?" Dustin said to the skater kid on the grass outside of Ravenna-Eckstein community center, slapping his hand with surprising nonchalance. The bud they received was dull green and furry-looking, reminding Lenny of the blotches of scuzzy mold that sometimes grew in bags of abandoned bread. They smoked it behind a dumpster on the back side of the community center, toking out of a pop can with a hole poked in the side. One of them crouched down while the other kept watch.

"Now that's some good shit," Dustin said after he had taken the first hit. "Not like the bammer weed homies usually be having."

"Word," Lenny agreed, crouching down to take the can.

He had only ever smoked weed once before, the day that he lost his virginity. That was before he met Dustin. Before they listened to Nas and Outkast in his friend's Laurelhurst house. Before they cut class to smoke bidis, shoplift CDs, and freestyle on the field where his dad used to hit him baseballs.

He flicked Dustin's lighter against the bud. Smoke coursed down his throat and lungs. He coughed and he coughed.

"Like I said," Dustin said. "This shit is the bomb."

Lenny leaned back against the green dumpster. He closed his eyes against the sky. His face felt extremely pale.

When he was able to see again, his friend was exhaling out of both nostrils, the smoke shooting down before rising to mingle with the wider air. They passed the can without speaking, the atmosphere between them beginning to hover and blur.

"You want to kick a beat for me real quick?" asked Lenny after the bowl had cashed.

"No doubt," Dustin said.

They pushed away from the dumpster into the field of gray grass. Lenny closed his eyes to focus his thoughts while Dustin began to cough a rickety beatbox into his fists.

"When the weed invades my brain," Lenny began, "it's like I'm entering a cave. I'm not talking about no rave, I mean a place that's safe. A respite from the strange, the days that never change…"

"Kick it, kid!" shouted Dustin between coughs.

"I grew up on a street with houses hidden behind hedges," Lenny rapped. "I used to climb up high to crawl on stone ledges. Even as a child I was enormously clever. Now when I rap, my rhymes be torrential."

Dustin coughed harder.

A river flowed inside of Lenny. It was suspended, immense. Each new rhyme was like the release of a stream.

*

For Lenny, it was a beginning. At the same time, his parents' marriage was on the verge of ending for good. Dinners were slapped together and silent. Then his dad announced that he was moving out.

"It was hella weird," Lenny said to Dustin the next day at Ravenna-Eckstein. "He just packed all of his shit into suitcases and loaded them into his car."

"Where'd he go to?" Dustin asked, focused on loading a bowl into the can.

"Some apartment," Lenny said. "Down near the airport."

Dustin looked up from the can. "Word? Why there?"

Lenny shrugged. "I have no idea."

And he never did understand why his father chose to move south when there were so many apartments for rent in the northeast. He knew that his father made less money as a middle school teacher than his mom did working as a nurse, but even a teacher should have been able to afford a better place to live than the one he ended up with.

On his first Friday with his dad, they drove south on the freeway towards Seatac while brake lights guttered and flashed. Near the airport they stopped at a sandwich shop in a strip mall next to a smoke shop and 7-11. While his dad fell into his meatball sub, Lenny watched the women through the window. There was a whole group of them smoking cigarettes and sipping Big Gulps and chewing gum and laughing. He watched them flick their cigarettes away and step into cars that visibly throbbed with bass.

Embarrassed, he looked down at his sub, glanced across the table at his father. His face looked bloated and garish in the restaurant's fluorescent glare.

*

At the Ravenna house, his mom was working evening shifts four nights a week. She left him notes on the butcher block paperclipped to ten dollar bills. He spent the cash on hamburgers from Kidd Valley or pizzas from Papa John's. He lit spliffs while he walked, letting the blend of tobacco and weed transport him into a state of splendor and ease. Secure in a mobile cocoon, he allowed himself to remember the way things used to be. Before the fights, the silences, and now the separation.

On one evening, he remembered something else—something that he had not thought about for years. One day, he had been at Magnuson Park with his parents when they sent him to throw away a bag of picnic trash. Reaching to discard the bag, he brushed his arm against an abandoned barbeque, which smoked his flesh like chicken breast. He staggered back to the beach while passing strangers regarded him strangely.

In the weeks after his parents' separation, this memory would return to him again and again.

*

He and Dustin began to spend most afternoons on the grass outside of the community center smoking weed and freestyling. A couple of other kids started to tag along. They were freckled and frail, but they beatbox all right and they always had a few bucks to throw down on a sack.

"My homies be down for the team, stay puffing that green, at times I wonder what my life actually means," rapped Lenny. "I got more bars than jail, make you feel like Braille, send messages like I'm delivering your mail."

Lenny loved the freestyle sessions. He could rhyme whatever he wanted as long as he was able to stay on the cypher's beat. He especially relished the moment right after he dropped a dope rhyme, when the other heads lit up, bodies convulsing as though possessed. In those moments he felt powerful. He felt warm.

Even the Seattle winter couldn't touch him when he flowed.

*

About a month after his parents' separation, he came home to find his mother seated at the kitchen table with a glass of white wine in front of her. Her cheeks were splotchy and red.

"I received a call from your school today, Leonard," she said.

He went past her to the refrigerator.

"It was about you missing class today. Apparently, you've been missing a lot of class lately."

He scanned for a can of root beer, found none. He chose a Capri Sun instead.

"You know what happens when you miss twelve classes, Lenny? You fail. You don't go on to the next semester."

Outside, dusk was beginning to fall. The grass, once a sprightly green, had turned dull and brown.

"Did you hear me, Lenny?"

"I'm not going to fail," he said softly.

"You don't know that." She shook her head. "I could tell that Dustin was going to be a bad influence. I could feel it."

"It's not Dustin, Mom. Maybe I'm not cut out for school. Maybe I'm not a school person."

"What kind of person are you, Lenny? A rap person?"

He shoved down a small smile.

"When we were your age," she said, "we sang for peace. We protested the war. We were trying to make things better."

"I'm so tired of hearing about the Sixties," he said.

"I'm worried about your future, Lenny."

"Yeah, well, I'm worried about yours."

There was a silence while his mother sought to compose herself.

"No more skipping class, Lenny," she finally said. "Do you hear me?"

"I heard you," he said.

*

Winter turned to spring, but the weather didn't change. Gray still clung to the city, impenetrable, persistent.

Meanwhile, Lenny and Dustin rapped. They had decided to form a hip-hop duo along the lines of Outkast or Gang Starr with Lenny serving as emcee and Dustin making beats. On weekend nights they crouched in one of Dustin's extra bedrooms. Lenny wrote rhymes in his black notebook while Dustin fiddled with a keyboard and computer.

"Days still dark but I'm trying to keep my left up," Lenny wrote. "Hone these skills one day to make a rent check. Two parent household, what I used to have. Two separate households, gotta pack a bag."

Sometimes during these sessions Lenny would allow himself to imagine a distant, beneficent future. He saw himself and Dustin standing before cameras while Andre or Guru or Nas praised their art to the world. And somewhere below them, made invisible by the lights, would be his parents, tears streaking their astonished, ruddy cheeks.

*

A few months after the divorce, a new face appeared on the community center grass. The kid walked up to the group without looking at anyone or offering a friendly word. He simply stood at the edge of the cypher with his gaze pointed at the ground.

After the mic was passed to him, his big shoulders straightened and his head began to dart.

"When the beat drops," he began, "I lay it all down on the line. Y'all don't want to hear it, but I'll speak it 'cause it's mine. The truth belongs to me like it was my pet. Keep on speaking until I get respect."

The cypher bucked its collective shoulders appreciatively.

"Today I was walking," the new rapper continued, "and I had myself a treat. All these white kids rapping like they from the street. But the truth is their hood about as lush as can be." He began to rap faster. "Corporate muthafuckas be colonizing like Columbus. The system's inhuman but we ain't never gonna discuss this. When you Richie Rich, the system runs fine, thanks. Now I'll pass the mic and let someone else assess this."

Lenny was transfixed, in thrall. He had never seen anything like this new rapper. His talent was genuine. His authority was unassailable.

*

"Hey, yo!" Lenny called as the cypher dispersed. "Wait up!"

The rapper turned to face him. His big shoulders were hunched again. His hands were packed into the pockets of his puffy coat.

"Lenny," Lenny said, putting out his hand.

The new rapper shook his hand formally, the way one might a parent's.

"Yo, man, you live around here?" Lenny asked.

"Hereabouts," the rapper said.

"That's dope, man. You know, because we're out here most days."

"All right," said the rapper.

"For real, man. Anytime you want to come through. I thought you brought a whole new element. A whole new dynamic."

The rapper smiled for the first time in a way that did not seem friendly. "What you mean by 'new'?" the rapper asked. "You mean 'new' like 'black'? You mean 'new' like that?"

"Nah, man," Lenny said, coloring, glancing down at the gray grass. "I meant your style, your flow. That shit was unique."

"So you liked all of that political shit," said the rapper, smiling wider.

"All I'm saying," Lenny said in a small voice, "is that we're out here most days."

"Don't worry, Lenny," the rapper said. "You'll see me again."

*

The next Friday, he rode south on the freeway towards Seatac while rain rapped against the windshield and a radio announcer droned on about the Iraq War.

He reached over to change the station. The car roared with the melodious raps of the Notorious B.I.G.

"I'm going, going, back, back, to Cali, Cali," Biggie sang.

Going, going, back, back, to Cali, Cali, Lenny echoed in his head.

"Where he's going?" his dad interrupted. "Indonesia?"

"California, Dad," Lenny said, turning up the volume.

When he got to the part about California being a great place to visit, Lenny had to restrain himself from shouting.

After the song ended, his dad spun down the sound.

"I'm sorry, but that doesn't sound like music to me. It sounds like an angry person shouting."

"He wasn't shouting," Lenny said. "He was singing."

"He sounded angry," his dad insisted.

Ahead of them, brake lights flared, darkened, and then flared again.

*

While they waited for their subs, Lenny watched the women through the window. All of them, he noticed, were black.

What had the rapper said to him that day at the community center? 'New' like black? 'New' like that? But he hadn't meant that. He admired his style. He envied his flow. He wished that he had been able to rap like that.

Maybe he couldn't, Lenny thought, looking down at the counter. What did he know about life on the streets? His dad was a science teacher. His mother was a nurse.

Then he felt for the scar on his forearm, remembered his walk over sand. He knew nothing about black experience, that was true. But he had his own pain. He had his own experience.

He thought of the black rapper from the community center. He realized that he had forgotten to ask his name.

Before Charlottesville

Days pass and the self
grows louder than before,
then slumps, sinks,
before rising again like a dog
who is irritated by an instinct
that something has gone wrong.

If I were a supremacist
I might believe in the superiority
of skin-on-skin,
a circumstance for which
I never found a name,
no matter how many
times you asked.
As though I were a god
who invented language.
As though I could
be that big.

On the day we learned
about Charlottesville,
I woke in the woods
wearing a suit and tie
with the words from
a wedding song
hollering through my head.
You are the best thing
that ever happened to me,
the song dripped.

Variations of Labor/ 79
Soon, the lyrics were
oozing through
my own booze-stained
lips, loud enough
to wake you next to me
in a zipped bag.

Later, I watched the video
of the sad-clown Nazi pleading
to his imagined people for respect
and became afraid—not at his
willingness to welcome skinlessness
but at mine, the cloudy-pink
wrapper of him merely a provocation
to the bloodthirst that lives inside
me along with whatever
remains constant beneath
this bag of brown,
its shade varying
by season and sun,
a husk I hold against you
in the bright light
after my brother's wedding
before we learned
about Charlottesville,
a circumstance for
which the only adequate
words are song.

Letter to an Old Friend

after Cesare Pavese

Boys will be boys
who have not
yet had to work.
And even then.
Even still.

The Incident at the Pizza Place

Danny rarely ate at The Pizza Place alone. His ten-dollar allowance only stretched so far. On the afternoon of the Incident, however, he did stop at The Pizza Place on his way home from the bus stop, going directly to the counter where slices had been laid out beneath heat lamps, ready to be transferred onto white ceramic plates or brown cardboard boxes, whichever the customer preferred. Danny planned to take his slice home and eat it in front of the TV before his parents got home from work and the three of them began their usual weeknightly routine that lately he had come to despise.

"You want it warmed up?" the counterworker asked, an older guy, at least twenty, with a t-shirt cut off at the sleeves.

Danny nodded, then watched the guy wriggle a slice out from a pie with tongs before sliding it into an oven in the back of the shop. A gust of heat tunneled towards him when the guy opened the oven door. He basked in its unexpected warmth before the guy snapped it closed.

Danny turned to find a seat. Five pairs of eyes stared back at him. The neighborhood crew. He looked away.

He knew them all by sight if not by name. They had ridden the school bus together in kindergarten. Then in first grade he transferred after testing into a program for students with advanced abilities. He had been riding a south to the Central District ever since.

"Hey," a pudgy boy with puffed up hair said to him now. "We were curious. Do you like black girls?"

Danny reddened and kept his eyes on the floor.

"It's okay if you do," the boy said teasingly. "Really. We won't judge."

Danny turned back to the counter, his fists balled at his waist. He wanted to smash their smirking faces.

*

Last year, he dated a black girl. She had been in the regular program, not the advanced. He had first seen her on a morning when they were both late to school. He had been putting his backpack away in his locker when he noticed a girl staring at him. He didn't know her—didn't know why she was staring.

Then at lunch another girl told him that the first girl liked the way his lips looked and wanted to know if he wanted to go out. He had barely remembered what the first girl looked like, but he told the second girl sure. He only ever had one girlfriend before and she dumped him for a more popular boy after just three days.

They hadn't seen much of each other, at first. They were in all different classes, since they were part of different academic programs, and they rode different school buses, since they lived on opposite ends of the city. Finally, after a few weeks, they agreed to meet at a movie theater downtown.

When they were seated, he swung his arm around her, which she seemed to like. After the movie started, he slid his hand down to her thigh, which caused her to shiver and shudder close in to his chest. He liked the way that felt—risky and safe all at the same time.

A week later, she called him when he was in his bedroom at home.

"You a bitch-ass punk for never calling me," she said, and in the background he could hear the other girl laugh.

The line clicked dead. A stinging sensation filled his chest. And he decided that he would never think about her again.

After the Incident at the Pizza Place, however, he did think about her. He was sorry that he had not gotten to know her well. He knew so little about her—what kind of movie theater candy she liked, where her brother went to high school, the name of the neighborhood where her grandparents lived. He had wanted to call her. He just hadn't been sure what to say.

The reality was that most of the kids in the advanced program lived north and were white. Most kids in the regular program lived south and were black. No one ever talked about it, but the social boundaries were clear.

There were a few exceptions. His friend Thomas, for example, who he met during the third grade. They had been on swim team together. Later, they did chess club. Every couple of weeks they slept over at each other's houses. Either he would go down to Columbia City where Thomas lived or Thomas would come up to Green Lake where he did. He liked sleeping over at Thomas's house because his parents would let them stay up late playing video games and their fridge was always stocked with cans of Mountain Dew.

He had known that Thomas was black, of course. And he knew that Thomas knew that he was white. But it didn't seem to be something that you were supposed to think about, let alone talk about out loud.

After the Incident at the Pizza Place, he could have told one of his other friends about what happened. Or he could have told his parents. But he didn't. He told Thomas.

*

"They said what?" Thomas asked, bouncing the ball firmly against the pavement.

They were shooting hoops outside of the portable where Mrs. Silverman taught them Spanish. The baskets had double rims, and there were cracks in the pavement where weeds poked through. But they preferred it to the main playground, which was always dominated by regular program kids.

"They asked if I liked black girls," Danny said, flushing slightly.

Thomas nodded once and tossed up a long jumper that spun off the rim.

"They can go fuck themselves," Danny called after his friend, who ran to retrieve the rebound. "They can fuck themselves hard."

Thomas didn't say anything as he skipped the ball across the pavement. Danny speared the pass with one hand, jutted his arms out to the side, and flung the ball from the middle of his chest. It went through.

"How many of them were there?" Thomas asked, bouncing him his change.

"I don't know," Danny said, readying the next shot. "Four or five?"

His next attempt was long, ricocheting off backboard and rim before bolting towards for a row of bushes. They were silent as they watched it roll.

"Let me come over tomorrow," Thomas said quietly. "We can see what's what."

*

Danny had never really seen Thomas get angry before. He was a shy, reserved kid who usually kept to himself. But he also had two sisters. He was probably thinking about them.

Not that there had not been plenty of opportunities for him to lose his temper over the years. During third grade, one of their classmates announced that kids from the regular program "smelled bad" before being furiously shushed by their teacher. In fifth grade, one girl dared another girl to kiss all of the boys' hands, which she did, all of them except Thomas's. And last year, during math class, their teacher mixed up Thomas with Jeremiah before moving on like nothing had happened while a bright flush crept up the side of her neck.

He and Thomas never spoke about these incidents. Instead,

they did their homework together. They played Madden on the Playstation in Thomas's basement. They shot hoops on the court with broken concrete and double rims.

*

The next afternoon, corner stores and barber shops gave way to restaurants and grocery stores and fancy boutique salons. Thomas stared out the window while Danny looked down at his shoes.

"What are we going to say to them?" Danny asked when he couldn't take the silence.

"I'm not going to say anything to them," Thomas said, still looking out the window.

"What are we going to do then?" Danny asked.

"We're going to see what's what," Thomas said with a small smile.

Danny lowered his head and jammed his knees up against the seat.

He had never been in a real fight before, he thought. He wasn't even sure that he would now how to throw a punch.

The Pizza Place was quiet when they entered. Even the wall-mounted televisions had been shut to mute.

"You want anything?" Danny asked his friend, setting his backpack on a table.

"I'm good," Thomas said, taking a seat that faced the door.

He went past him to the counter. He found the same worker as last time hovering above the same four types of pies. The only difference was the worker's expression. It held not quite an accusation, not quite a complaint, but it contained aggression. It caused Danny to look away.

"What you need, man?" the guy said softly.

"A slice of cheese," Danny said, studying the jars of oregano on the counter.

"For here or to go?" the guy asked.

"For here," Danny said.

"I'll bring it out. To you and your friend."

Danny nodded and retreated to his seat.

He had nearly finished the slice when the neighborhood crew came through the doors all loud banter and swinging backpack and curly, poofed-up hair. After they saw Thomas and Danny, their chatter ceased. There was satisfaction in watching their comfort collapse.

They sauntered without speaking across the room. Then the pudgy boy turned.

"What up, gangstas?" he called in a shrill voice.

The other kids laughs.

"What'd you say?" Thomas asked as he rose from his seat.

"I was greeting you," the kid said, smirking.

"You want to greet me outside?"

The kid shrugged. "If you do."

"Let's go then," Thomas said.

One by one, the neighborhood kids filed out. All it took was one push. The pudgy boy stepped forward. Thomas rushed to meet him. Then the neighborhood boy was tumbling backward as his feet flew out from underneath him.

What now, motherfuckers? thought Danny. What now?

Then he saw Thomas's face. He did not look triumphant or thrilled. He looked disoriented. He looked scared.

Danny stepped forward and wrapped his arms around his friend's chest.

"C'mon, man," he whispered. "Let's get out of here."

Thomas shrugged him off. "Fuck these motherfuckers," he said in a strained voice. "Anyone else want a piece of me?"

No one did. They walked south from the pizza place in the direction of Danny's house. Rain punched down at them. They pulled their hoods over their heads.

It had been a mistake bringing Thomas here, Danny thought.

That hadn't been his friend's fight. He wasn't even sure that it was his.

When they got home, he would ask him about the incidents at their school. If he wanted to talk, he would listen. If he didn't, that was fine, too.

The Pizza Place had been his special place, he thought. The place where he went for birthday parties and after Little League games and on nights when his mom was too tired to cook.

He and Thomas marched, together and apart, beneath a changing sky. Behind them, the pizza place receded from view.

To Feel Inspired

Blue lights flash
through the bare window,
flicker like the laptop screen
pointed towards our face.
The body
springs up.
The body knows
what to do.
The body bangs
head, neck
craned to see.

Downstairs neighbor
shakes shoulders against
open apartment door.
Dead body behind building.
No way he can sleep
until it's been removed.

Nothing to say
or see here
for the body—
mine.
It does not know
this man.

Upstairs, hand
pushes laptop up,
punches buttons

until it begins
to speak.
A convention on—
chirping mouths
in quivering heads
to fill our ears
with air.
An election on
and we want to feel
inspired.

Triumph

I always forget
who lives
in my city.
No comment
on them,
my memory's bad.
Or good
for certain things.
Like faces
or the items
on a grocery list
or the precise feelings
a book produced
in me once,
although perhaps not
its phrases or ideas.
But people,
you lovely impenetrables,
too often I forget
you exist.
It is not difficult
to reach out
to you in moments,
to recognize your flesh
and flutter as mine.
Still, the grocery list
lengthens.
Somewhere a party

commences.
I reserve sympathy
for myself
inside myself.
I don't know if this is a triumph
of compassion or greed
but I guard it like passion
or grief.

Take Me Out to the Ballgame

"You know people don't look like this anywhere else?" Nathan said to his friend outside Safeco Field.

"How's that?" Tom said, puffing his smoke.

"The beards," Nathan said, gesturing to the crowd. "The hoodies. The flannel shirts."

"It's a pioneer town."

"Actually," Nathan said, "in Brooklyn, people look like this. The hipsters do. But more stylish. More put together."

Tom shrugged, huffing his Marlboro Light.

"C'mon, man," Nathan said, shifting feet. "Let's go in. The game's about to start."

*

Nathan had been away from Seattle for twelve years. During that time, he came back once a year to visit family and friends, but he had not thought about the city then. He had not lived there anymore, and he did not plan on living there again. Seattle was a middling place, he might have thought, more hinterlands than metropolis, which would have been fine had it not been for the provincialism and self-regard that made its residents insufferable.

So he might have thought had he taken the time to consider, which he had not, since he had been busy during his twenties. He had worked hard in New York and done reasonably well. After Columbia, he interned for a national magazine, which led to a paid staff position there. The contacts he made then allowed him to launch out on his own.

It was Deidre who brought him back—Deidre who decided that Seattle was where she wanted to live. They both were about to turn thirty, she wanted to start a family, and living close to his parents, she thought, would provide a huge help. Her own parents lived in northern Florida and were boozing Republicans. Seattle had the added advantage of placing three thousand miles between them.

She applied for and was soon offered a marketing position at a company in South Lake Union. He connected with an advertising agency downtown. With help from his parents, they were able to make a down payment on a condo overlooking the Pike/Pine corridor—not a desirable part of town when he was younger but now a location that seemed to be right at the center of things.

Whatever reticence he felt about moving back to his hometown was assuaged by the fact that he barely recognized it anymore. So much had changed. So much was new. On a Lyft ride to his gym one afternoon, his driver told him that she liked working for the company because it helped to refamiliarize her with a city that she no longer felt she knew.

Far from saddening him, this confidence brought him comfort. The past was only past. There was little danger of its return.

*

He saw his old friends before they recognized him. Baseball hats turned backwards. Puffy, waterproof vests.

He could not help but grin.

"Nathan!" Jim said.

"Jimbo!" he replied.

They wrapped each other in a hug. Here was something that he had missed in New York—men who were unafraid to press their bodies into his.

"Need a beer?" Jim asked after he was settled. "I was about to head down for a round."

"Sure," Nathan said, tugging his wallet from pocket.

"No, no." Jim waved him off.

"I insist," Nathan said, fanning out three twenties.

Jim studied the bills. "Well, if you put it that way…"

"I do," Nathan said, patting him gently on the back.

"Anyone else want a beer?" Jim called down the row. "Nathan's buying."

"Me," Colin said.

"Me, too," said Jamie.

"I'll go down with you," Tom said. "I forgot I have to drop the kids off at the pool."

They all laughed.

Here was something that he had not missed—his old friends' puerility, their juvenescence.

"So what's going on with the M's these days?" Nathan asked after Tom and Jim had gone.

"Stupid Mariners," Jamie muttered, staring at his phone. "They're hitting now, but their pitching is no good. Once their pitching picks up, their hitting'll probably fall off. It's been that kind of year."

"Disagree," Colin said, shaking his head. "I very much disagree. I think they still have a chance. The main problem is that they've been terrible in one-run games. If they can revert even to league average in just that one category, they're right there with Texas competing for first place."

"All right, Moneyball," Jamie said, looking up at his friend with contempt. "Keep on trying to impress Nathan with that sabermetric shit. The truth is they're nine games out of the Wild Card. Not even the division. The Wild Card!"

"You remember '95?" Colin said. "They were twelve games out in August. What happened then?"

"That was twenty years ago!"

Nathan leaned back in his seat. He wished that he had bought garlic fries on his way if only so that he had something to do with his hands.

"You a Yankees fan, Nathan? After all of that time in New York?"

"No—" He had been going to say that he hadn't followed professional sports in years. But he caught himself just in time. "More of a Mets fan than anything else."

"The Mets are pretty dope," Jamie said.

"Anyone but the Yankees," Colin said.

"The Yankees can suck a dick," Jamie said.

They both laughed.

*

He had always been different than them. It was not only that he preferred to read chapter books in the dugout while they competed in the games on the field or that he was compelled by travel while they liked to stay close to home or that they absorbed the ideas passed down to them from television while he was interested in learning how to think for himself. Or it was all of those things and none of them, some essential difference that had never really dimmed.

Even so, they had made him feel like a full-fledged member of their crew. It was a shock to them when he left, but it couldn't have been much of a surprise. Of the twelve colleges to which he applied, only Whitman, in Walla Walla, was in Washington state. The rest were scattered haphazardly across the country, the only criterion he used that they offer substantial financial aid. When Columbia not only accepted him but offered him a generous scholarship to boot, he had not had to think twice.

During the first few years, they kept up through text message, voicemail, and the occasional e-mailed photograph. (This was before Facebook, before Twitter). During his junior year of college, when he started working nights in the Greek restaurant in Morningside Heights for extra spending money, he became too busy to communicate and the distance between them grew.

But it was not only that he became too busy. It was also that he had developed different priorities. When he was younger, he had wanted to meet people who cared as much about culture and history as his old friends did about what happened on the field. And in New York he had met such people. They were aspiring journalists and filmmakers and poets, the sons and daughters of professors and businessmen and politicians. They knew the right people, so then he knew the right people.

He worked hard during his twenties and did reasonably well.

*

"Beer, beer, beer, and beer," said Jim, passing down cups.

"Thanks, Jim," said Jamie.

"You should thank Nathan," Jim said.

"Thanks, Nathan," said Jamie.

"No worries," Nathan said.

They each butted plastic cups.

The Mariners were playing the Orioles, a middling team, Nathan read that morning online. Their only bright spot was their center fielder, who, years ago, used to playe for Seattle. The M's had traded him during a stretch run for a pitcher who was supposed to help them make the playoffs; instead, the pitcher underperformed, the Mariners missed the postseason, and the center fielder went on to become a once-in-a-generation star.

That last part he had not read. It was the strange the details that lodged in the memory.

"How's it being back?" Jim asked as the Mariners' second baseman, a player Nathan didn't recognize, stepped up to the plate.

"Oh, not bad," Nathan said, watching the Orioles' pitcher's fastball veer outside. "A little cold, maybe. But overall it's been good."

"Cold? For real? After all your time in New York?"

"Well, but New York had seasons," Nathan said. "Yes, it was cold in the wintertime, but then it got hot during the summer. Here, it's the same damn gray all of the time."

"You said cold," Jim pointed out.

Nathan blushed, reaching for his beer. "It does feel cold. I don't know why. Maybe all the moisture in the air?"

"That that's why right-handed hitters don't like playing here," Colin put in. "The cold marine air knocks their flies straight down."

"I didn't know that," Nathan said, even though he did.

"You remember Richie Sexson?" Colin said.

"Goddamned Sexson," Jamie muttered, looking at his phone.

"People love to pick on Sexson," said Tom, "but Beltre was just as bad."

"Look at what he's doing now for Texas," said Jim.

"He's raking for Texas," agreed Tom.

"Stupid Mariners," said Jim.

"Stupid goddamned Mariners," Jamie said.

*

If Nathan had been successful in certain areas, he had been less able in others. His triumphs had been mainly professional and reputational. In the field of personal relationship, he fared less well.

Oh, he had made friends—prim, upper-middle class professionals who he accompanied to brunch and dinner parties and music shows in Williamsburg on the weekends. They had worn the uniforms of their class privilege—crisp Oxford shirts, handmade European loafers, t-shirts designed to look like they were old. He had eventually learned to wear those clothes, too, but always with trepidation. Every morning he had been worried that he would eventually be found out.

There had been women—enough woman during his time away that it would have shocked his friends from home. But most often he had been drunk and later on ashamed. Deirdre had been the first woman who he met in New York who he could really talk to, who he wanted to stay sober with, who he felt, ultimately, that he was able to trust. When he first met her, she was all overpowering perfume and ostentatious make-up and precarious high heel. But there was something strange about her, too, something off-kilter and out of place, that attracted him to her immediately.

They had dated in New York for four years, then traveled, lived abroad. With Deirdre, he had felt at home, but also that he was travelling somewhere new.

*

Neither team had scored after five innings, exactly the kind of pitcher's duel that he would have enjoyed back when he followed the sport. Now he found it dull.

"I heard you guys bought a place," Jim said as the Orioles catcher took a pitch outside.

"Yeah," Nathan said. "A little place. It's only eight hundred square feet. Two bedrooms, one bath."

"Where?" Tom asked.

"Capitol Hill," he said.

"You must like hipsters."

"Nah." Nathan blushed. "It's just that Deirdre works in South Lake Union and we thought that it'd be good to be close to downtown. How about you guys? Where you living these days?"

"I'm in Greenwood near the old Fred Meyer," Jim said.

"Jamie and I are in Ballard," said Colin.

"And I'm living at home right now," Tom said in a pained voice. "Trying to put some money away."

"Rents in this city have gotten really crazy," Nathan said.

"It's ridiculous," said Jim. "Studios up near where I live go for twelve or thirteen hundred."

"It's all the tech money coming in," said Colin. "Amazon and Microsoft."

"Google and Facebook, too," Jamie said.

"Doesn't your wife work for tech company, Nathan?" Tom asked.

"More of a…marketing firm," Nathan said. "They do sometimes work with tech companies."

The Orioles shortstop fouled a pitch into the net.

"We need to have you guys over," Nathan said. "We just got a TV. We can cook up some burgers and watch a game."

Just then, a loud crack sent the ball shooting high against the night sky. As it descended, it grew closer. Please, Nathan thought, gripping his chair, do not let that ball land here.

Then the center fielder slowed and raised his glove above his head. Ball slapped against leather with an audible thwap.

"Thank God," Jim said, sinking back into his seat.

Colin slapped Nathan's shoulder. "The moisture in the air!"

*

When Deirdre suggested that they move home, his initial reaction had been negative. He had left Seattle for reasons that were important to him; once gone, he had felt little need to look back. In Seattle, he had always been strange. Analytical. He had been the type that thought too much. In New York, during college and the years after, he had been a person of purpose, interests, and ideas.

Over time, however, he warmed to the notion. He and especially Deirdre were exhausted by the high rents and relentless crowds and logistical strain of New York. The thought of raising a child in such an environment was difficult to fathom.

Seattle really was a nice place. The air was clean, the water pure. It had great hiking and good food. There was plenty of economic opportunity, too, not only inside the big tech companies but also among all the ancillary operations.

Or so Deirdre had repeated during her months-long campaign. When Nathan imagined Seattle, all that he could see was gray clouds, the dismal site of his childhood and dreary adolescence. In New York, he had an adult identity that had been developed and tested over time. Seattle was the place that identity had formed in reaction to—provincial, mediocre, supremely pragmatic. To move back would be to acknowledge defeat—or so he had always thought.

For months, his wife insisted. Eventually, he gave in.

*

After the Orioles made the last out of the seventh inning, Jim went down for another round. Nathan stood to sing with his old friends.

"Take me out to the ballgame…" the PA announcer began.

As a little white ball danced frenetically on the screen, darkness settled at the edges of his vision. It was a feeling that he associated with chilly mornings walking to the bus stop before school and overcast afternoons holed up in his bedroom at home.

"Take me out with the crowd…" his friends sang.

The darkness deepened, blurring his sight. He brought his fingers to his temples, digging into the skin.

"Buy me some peanuts and Cracker Jack…" the stadium bellowed.

Had it been a mistake coming back? he wondered, clamping his eyes shut. Here, at the ballgame, it was like the last twelve years did not exist. Like all of the progress he made had instantly been reversed.

"Root, root, for the Mariners…" the city roared.

He felt a hand on his shoulder and turned. Jim, breathing heavily, thrust a carton into his hands.

"I got you garlic fries," he said with a grin.

Nathan glanced down at the yellow mound. Garlic fries. He looked up at his friend.

"Tom said they were your favorite," Jim said.

His favorite. Years ago. He smiled. Another lifetime. Wasn't it? It was hard for him to tell.

He lifted a single fry from the carton and laid it against his tongue.

Of Two Minds

Not silence or erasure
but the radical assertion
of the mind,
of some consciousness beyond
one's ability to arrange
the self's thoughts and emotions
into structures that have
been pre-arranged, pre-accepted
by collective habits
of obedience and deferral.
Not insane
but of course insane.
No shame
but of course shame.
The first mind wanting to be received
and cast under
the mantle of safety.
The second resistant
to all notions of safety,
repellant to the other,
perhaps all
others.

Or perhaps not.
Perhaps the pairing
simply regrettable,
the second mind lost

in individual pursuit.
Or both minds lost,
both desiring that grace
that comes
with intuitive presence.
Both wanting
to unite.
Both
    to lift

In Starbucks on my Thirty

I.
I don't mean to be crass
but these dark chocolate
peanut butter cups taste
really fucking good.
Last night I ate too many
movie theater Swedish Fish
and the difference this morning
impresses itself upon me.
I get a little weepy
thinking about it, actually,
although that may
have more to do with poor K.
face-diving
onto the express lanes
last week
or G.'s cancer
or the general, tawdry
fucked-up state of things.
Last week, I started reading poems
again, which I take
to be a good sign.
At their best, poems stir things
in me, which is better, I feel,
than walking around dead.
Mostly these days, I find

myself taking care of business
which is fine—
I spent a long time
getting up late
and walking around thinking
about what I was going to make
myself for lunch.
Fifteen minutes ago, I sat down.
Fifteen minutes from now,
I have to go back
to work, less than that, even,
if I don't want to be late.
I don't not want to be late
but I don't want another
attendance point, either,
which is the whole purpose
of the system, I guess,
motivating you with fear.
It doesn't feel like fear
when I'm at work, though.
It feels like a manager's wink.
Like, "Hey, buddy.
Would you mind
picking that piece of trash
up off the floor?"
I remember Adorno's idea
about pop culture, how fans don't understand
that they are enjoying the sound
of their own alienation
reflected back at them.
T., over in Bakery,
likes that idea, too.

II.
Likes that idea, too,

but to what extent
I don't know
since I have only begun
to get to know him
as I have only begun
to know nearly everyone
who I think I know,
even you, dear reader, who I imagine
surrounded by strangers
who you believe are unlike you.
I am wary of the individual.
I am wary of the individual
yet I recognize the importance
of two hands and one heart,
of ankles that swell
and a stomach that burns.
When I lay my hand down on
my wife's thigh at night,
I don't always picture the chickens
that have been left too long
in the deli hot case,
but sometimes I do.
The truth is that I take satisfaction
in breaking down
those broken birds,
that I feel affinity
for the carcasses
that have been consigned
to my care.
At home, I tell my vegetarian friends
that I admire them,
and I do, I think, sneaking mouthfuls
of boiled bird
from the walk-in freezer.
I am a dissolute

and undisciplined creature,
but I harbor no illusions
that I am alone.

III.
No illusions
that I am alone
in Starbucks on my thirty
writing on the back
of a brown pastry bag
given to me by a barista
who was oddly quiet for this Starbucks
when he turned his back on me
to pour my small, dark drip.
Would it be too much to say
that I felt for him a kinship?
Would it be unreasonable to think
that I experienced his emotions
as my own?
When he turned to me
his face was pale,
the paleness of horror
but also light.

IV.
The paleness of horror
but also light,
I think in Starbucks again
on my thirty,
the barista from last week
fired or dead
or on his day off at home,
earbuds plugging his head.
Yesterday I found out that G. died
on my fifteen and was not prepared

for the sadness that pinned my shoulders back,
held them there like a mental patient's straitjacket.
All around me my co-workers chatted and snacked

and played card games on their phones.
I thought of how little I knew of them
despite all of the time that we spent together
and there was further sadness in that—
the notion that if I were to speak then
I would have had nothing to say.
I closed my eyes and was a child again
over at G.'s house for dinner, the table
set and spread.
Lonely, aggrieved men
shivered their thoughts
through the speakers.
My parents and their friends
nodded their heads.
How miraculous,
how unimaginable, nearly,
to have been a child
who believed that laughter
and communal feeling
were human beings' natural state.

The Mountain

"Would you take a look at that mountain?" my dad used to yell when I was young, braking hard enough that the cars behind us would honk. He never used Rainier's proper name. For my father, the mountain was a marvel without parallel or peer.

The thing of it was on those rare, cloudless afternoons in spring, the mountain did have company. It did have competition. Turn west and the Olympic Range skated across the sky in its low, wordless scrawl. Look east and the Cascade Range loomed over townships as fragile and ephemeral as Legos. But for my father it didn't matter. The mountain had an aura that was all its own.

It sometimes seemed as though he felt personally responsible for the mountain's existence. And in a way now I think that he was—responsible for the mountain's presence in his own life, at least, and in our lives. It had taken a certain amount of audacity to leave the small town in Pennsylvania where he was from for a region of the country where such extravagances of nature are nearly ordinary.

Driving to baseball practice or school, I would hunch over in the passenger seat with a book until he cuffed my shoulder and crowed at the top of his lungs, "Would you take a look at that mountain?" I would groan and go back to my book.

I was a city kid. Schooled in crowded classrooms, bussed down busy arterials, I ran free in concrete-and-dirt respites called city parks, found my own forms of sustenance in books and ballparks and movie theaters.

Nature. The word used to make me shudder. Nature meant

cross-country skiing, that demented family Christmas tradition that succeeded only in confirming my antipathy towards all things white (mayonnaise, tartar sauce, snow). Nature meant family "drives" one Sunday a month to watch tulips grow, or fill bins with blueberries, or harass some unwitting Canadian for directions to a suitably nature-like destination.

Nature meant hikes. How I hated them! Hikes represented all that was mysterious to me about the world—and all that was incomprehensible about my parents. The fact that people would drive hours away from the city to traipse around areas that were plentiful with plants that poked and wild animals that bit struck me as lunacy, an entirely masochistic affair.

For most of my life I did not see the mountain. Rainier may have recalled the natural beauty mostly missing from my father's city life, but, for me, the mountain was only an outsized reminder of the differences between us.

It took a long time before I was able to look.

CPSIA information can be obtained
at www.ICGtesting.com
Printed in the USA
BVHW042029260319
543769BV00011B/46/P

9 781634 059770